The Things I **Love** About
Grandparents

Trace Moroney

The Five Mile Press

I **love** my grandparents . . .
and – I have four of them to love
. . . and who love me!

They are: Grandma and Grandpa
(who are my mum's mother and father),

and Oma and Opa
(who are my dad's mother and father).

My grandparents are a part of my *family*.

Grandma and Grandpa live close by
and I love to visit them almost every day.
They make me feel really special.

Grandma likes
to teach me
how to knit . . .

and, lets me
dress up in her
old clothes and
jewellery . . .

and we bake cookies together while we laugh and talk about all sorts of things.

Grandpa likes to teach me how to build things . . .
and, he shares lots of funny stories about the
things he liked to do when he was my age . . .
and . . . he always forgets where he
has put his glasses!

Grandma and Grandpa are really, **really** old and, really, **really** wrinkly!

They also have a really old, wrinkly dog called Biscuit, and a really old, wrinkly cat called Mouse.

I find it hard to imagine that Grandma and Grandpa used to be the same age as me.

They say they still feel really young on the **inside** but their bodies have just grown older on the **outside** – and just don't work as well.

Sometimes they find it hard to do the simple
things that they love . . . like gardening.
So, I really love to help them . . . and I learn
lots of fun and interesting things too!

I love Oma and Opa too.
They live a long way away . . . so I don't
see them very often.
But, we do spend a lot of time talking on
the phone, or sending letters and photos
by email or post.

This helps me get to know them, and they love to know about me — how much I am growing, the things I am learning, the friends that I have, and my thoughts and feelings.

Sharing time with my grandparents
helps me feel happy and secure and loved.
I **love** being with them and they
love being with me.

I **love** my grandparents!

Notes for Parents and Caregivers

'The Things I Love' series shares simple examples of creating **positive thinking** about everyday situations our children experience.

A positive attitude is simply the inclination to generally be in an optimistic, hopeful state of mind. Thinking positively is not about being unrealistic. Positive thinkers recognise that bad things can happen to pessimists and optimists alike – however, it is the positive thinkers who *choose* to focus on the hope and opportunity available within every situation.

Researchers of positive psychology have found that people with positive attitudes are more creative, tolerant, generous, constructive, successful and open to new ideas and new experiences than those with a negative attitude. Positive thinkers are happier, healthier, live longer, experience more satisfying relationships, and have a greater capacity for love and joy.

I have used the word **love** numerous times throughout each book, as I think it best describes the *feeling* of living in an optimistic and hopeful state of mind, and it is a simple but powerful word that is used to emphasise our positive thoughts about people, things, situations and experiences.

Grandparents

Grandparenting is a wonderful opportunity to be playful and share memories, hobbies and activities with a young and inquisitive grandchild and to teach a positive attitude toward ageing.

Whether you are a full-time grandparent (actively involved in rearing your grandchildren), a companionate grandparent (whose focus is on sharing playful activities and interactions), a remote grandparent (who lives far away) or a step-grandparent, there is no denying that the role of being a grandparent is one of great importance and meaning to both grandparents and grandchildren.

A grandparent can play different roles, such as that of the family historian, mentor, surrogate parent, role model, nurturer – all while providing love, support, comfort, guidance and encouragement within the family framework.

Trace Moroney

*My mother said that if she knew how much fun
grandchildren were, she would have had them first!*

Dare to Love

The Five Mile Press Pty Ltd
1 Centre Road, Scoresby
Victoria 3179 Australia
www.fivemile.com.au
Part of the BonnierPublishing Group
www.bonnierpublishing.com
Illustrations and text copyright © Trace Moroney, 2011
All rights reserved
www.tracemoroney.com
First published 2011
This edition 2013
Printed in China 5 4 3 2 1
National Library of Australia Cataloguing-in-Publication entry
Moroney, Trace
The things I love about grandparents / Trace Moroney.
9781742487090 (hbk.)
9781742487083 (pbk.)
For pre-school age.
Grandparents--Juvenile literature. Love--Juvenile literature.
306.8745